CHEW ON THIS!

BY SUSAN DEVINS
DESIGNED BY JERRI JOHNSON • ILLUSTRATED BY SAN MURATA

SOMERVILLE HOUSE, USA

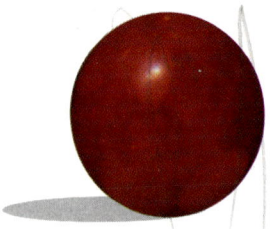

Read these fabulous gum facts and then make your own chewing gum!

Includes a kit with easy-to-follow instructions and everything you'll need to make yummy fruit-flavored gum.

After you make a batch of gum you can make your own gum wrappers — invent your own brand names and come up with neat shapes!

So go ahead... **CHEW ON THIS!**

Copyright © 1998 by Somerville House Books Limited.
Images copyright © 1998 Photodisc, Inc. Images copyright © 1998 Image Ideas Inc. Image copyright © 1998 Phototone Inc.

All rights reserved. No part of this publication may be reproduced, stored in any retrieval system, or transmitted in any form or by any means, electronic, mechanical, photocopying, recording, or otherwise without the prior permission of the publisher.

ISBN: 1-58184-007-1 ABCDEFGHIJ

Printed in Canada

Somerville House, USA is distributed by Penguin Putnam Books for Young Readers, 345 Hudson Street, NY, 10014
Published in Canada by Somerville House Publishing, a division of Somerville House Books Limited, 3080 Yonge Street, Suite 5000, Toronto, Ontario M4N 3N1

First Edition 10 9 8 7 6 5 4 3 2 1

CHOMP! SNAP! POP!

Chomp! Thwack! Smack! Pop! Crack!
That's the sound of millions of smiling people around the world chomping and gnawing on chewing gum!

It's fun to chew! It moistens the mouth, sweetens the breath, and is a jolly between-meals treat. For a quick bolt of energy, pop a stick into your mouth. You can blow bubbles, blow double bubbles, or crack gum. If you fly in an airplane, you can chew gum to unplug your ears. And if you get a little nervous, you can stick a wad in your mouth to calm down.

Chewing gum is everywhere! There are 550 chewing gum companies in 93 countries around the world. People chew more than 100,000 tons (90,000 t) of gum every year — that's enough to make a sculpture of a cruise ship out of gum!

WHAT OTHER PEOPLE CHEW

Peru and Bolivia
Indians chew coca leaves, which grow on bushes at high elevations. They put together a wad of 30 to 35 leaves and chew it into a pulpy mess. Coca is said to drive evil forces from the fields. Some witch doctors use it in healing.

Yemen
People put as many coarse green leaves called "gat" into their mouths as they can and chew them.

India
Betel leaves, or "paan," are chewed as an after-dinner treat. The leaves are quite astringent and are used as a breath freshener. Sometimes the leaves are stuffed with betel nuts, rose petals preserved in syrup, cardamom, and coconut.

Thailand
People chew both betel leaves and "miang," which are fermented tea leaves.

Africa
People chew frankincense, a gum resin that is often used in incense.

Saskatchewan
Farm kids chew ears of wheat.

THE WIDE WORLD OF GUM!

Arab world	Elki
Latin America & Spain	Goma de mascar
Australia	Chewing gum
Austria	Kaugummi
Canada (French)	Gomme à mâcher
China	Heung how chu
France	Le chewing gum
Germany	Kaugummi
Greece	Tsikles
India	Chewing gum
Italy	La gomme da masticare
Japan	Gamu
Malaysia	Shee yung tung
Norway	Tyggegummi
Philippines	Chewing gum
Portugal	Pastilka elastica
Russia	Zhevatelnaya rezinka
Sweden	Tuggummi
Switzerland	Chaetschgummi
Thailand	Mag farang

FUN FACTS

- IN THE CZECH REPUBLIC, GUM CHEWING IS CALLED "ZVYKACKA" — WHICH TRANSLATES INTO "CUD CHEWING"!

- JAPANESE CHEMISTS INVENTED MOOD GUM, WHICH CHANGES COLORS WHEN YOU'RE HAPPY, SAD, ANGRY, AND SO ON. THE CHANGE TAKES PLACE WHEN THE ACIDITY LEVEL IN A PERSON'S SALIVA RISES OR FALLS.

- CHEWING THE LEAVES OF AN INDIAN PLANT NAMED "GYMNEMA SYLVESTRE" TAKES AWAY THE TONGUE'S ABILITY TO TASTE ANYTHING SWEET FOR A COUPLE OF HOURS AND MAKES SUGAR TASTE LIKE SAND.

- SAN LUIS OBISPO, CALIFORNIA, IS THE SITE OF BUBBLE GUM ALLEY. IT'S A SMALL ALLEY ABOUT SIX FEET (2 M) WIDE WITH TWO-STORY BRICK WALLS ABSOLUTELY COVERED WITH ABC (ALREADY-BEEN-CHEWED) GUM WADS!

- "GUMSUCKER" IS A SLANG EXPRESSION MEANING AN AUSTRALIAN AND COMES FROM AUSTRALIAN CHILDREN'S HABIT OF SUCKING GUM FROM THE EUCALYPTUS TREE.

A BRIEF TIME LINE OF CHEWING GUM HISTORY

A.D. 50
Ancient Greeks chewed a gummy substance called "mastiche" (mas-TEE-ka) from the bark of the mastic tree. Greek women used it to sweeten their breath. In fact, the English word "masticate," meaning "to chew," comes from the word "mastiche."

A.D. 200
The Mayans, a large group of Central American Indians, chewed chicle, the latex from the sapodilla tree found in the area's rain forests.

FUN FACT: The Mayans often used chicle to make rubber shoes or galoshes. They dipped their bare feet into the goo. The latex then hardened to the shape of their feet.

1600s
When the colonists settled in North America in present-day New England, the Wampanoag Indians introduced them to chewing the resin of the spruce tree.

1848
John Curtis of Bradford, Maine, made the first commercial spruce gum product, "State of Maine Pure Spruce Gum." It was a hot seller until spruce trees were used for something else: making newspapers.

1869
William F. Semple, an Ohio dentist, decided that gum was ideal for jaw exercises. He invented a gum that used rubber as its base. Semple added "scouring properties" such as chalk, powdered licorice root, and charcoal. He filed the first ever patent for chewing gum, but he never sold the gum commercially.

WHY CAN'T YOU EVER FIND A SINGLE STICK OF GUM?
THEY ALWAYS MOVE IN PACKS.

WHAT DO YOU GET WHEN YOU CROSS A TEAM OF SKY DIVERS WITH A PACK OF GUM?
GUM DROPS.

WHAT DO YOU CALL A GRIZZLY WITH BUBBLE GUM STUCK ON ITS FUR?
A GUMMI BEAR.

1869

Remember the Alamo? Modern chewing gum owes its existence to a lucky meeting between Mexican general Antonio López de Santa Anna, the conqueror of the Alamo, and Thomas Adams Sr., a U.S. inventor. In 1869 Santa Anna was in exile on Staten Island near New York City. He was broke. He tried to sell the idea of using chicle as a rubber substitute to Adams, who tried to vulcanize chicle (improve its mechanical properties by treating it with sulfur and heat). When that didn't work, he happened to walk into a drugstore and noticed a little girl asking for a penny's worth of paraffin gum. He remembered that his buddy Santa Anna was always chewing the very chicle he was trying to sell. Adams tested it and found out it was smoother and more chewable than all other gum bases then available. He made a batch and convinced the druggist to carry Adams New York Gum No.1.

1871

Thomas Adams Sr. devised the first patented gum-making machine, which broke the gum off into penny lengths. He zipped up the taste by adding first sassafras and then a licorice flavor. Today Adams Black Jack is the oldest flavored gum on the market.

1886
William J. White, a popcorn salesman, discovered that mixing flavors with corn syrup before adding it to the chicle made the flavor last longer. His peppermint Yucatan Gum became a big hit.

1888
In the U.S., the first practical vending machine appeared. It dispensed chewing gum on the elevated train platforms in New York City.

1890–1893
William Wrigley Jr., a clever baking-powder salesman, changed his product line to chewing gum and made recognizable brand names through clever advertising campaigns. Newspapers, magazines, posters, and trolley cars carried his messages. Spearmint and Juicy Fruit gum became best-sellers.

William Wrigley Jr. sent his gum business into the stratosphere by mailing a stick of gum to everyone who was listed in all 1915 U.S. telephone books.

1898
Beeman's gum was originally invented as a cure for heartburn.

1899
Franklin V. Canning invented Dentyne, which was sold as the first dental gum. "Prevents decay, sweetens breath," read the package. The gum's name is a contraction of "dental" and "hygiene."

1900
Henry Fleer invented the first candy-coated gum, inspired by candy-coated almonds, which were popular at the time. He named his gum "Chiclets," after chicle latex.

1906
Bubble gum was invented by Henry Fleer's brother, Frank. His Blibber–Blubber didn't sell well because it was too sticky and wasn't good for blowing bubbles.

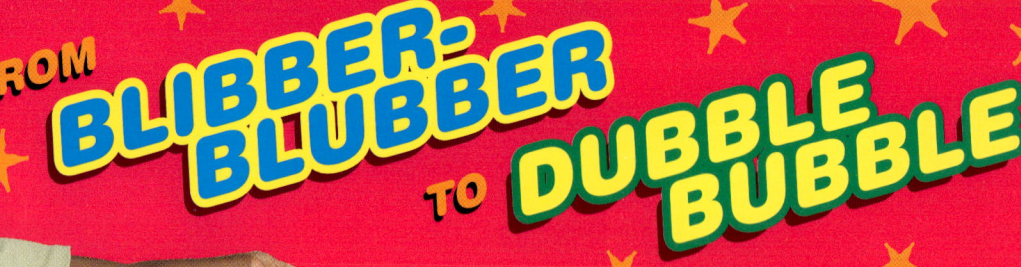

FROM BLIBBER-BLUBBER TO DUBBLE BUBBLE

FRANK H. FLEER POPPED OUT THE FIRST BUBBLE GUM PRODUCT IN 1906. HE CALLED IT "BLIBBER-BLUBBER." UNFORTUNATELY, IT DIDN'T MAKE IT AS A BUBBLE BLOWER — IT STUCK TO FACES AND CLOTHING, AND IT WAS TOO WET TO BLOW.

TWENTY-TWO YEARS LATER WALTER DIEMER, A KEEN YOUNG COST ACCOUNTANT FROM THE FLEER CORPORATION, HIT UPON THE MAGIC BATCH ON AN EARLY AUGUST MORNING IN 1928.

HIS OFFICE JUST HAPPENED TO BE NEXT TO THE LAB AND HE STARTED EXPERIMENTING WITH RUBBER BASES. SOME OF THEM BUBBLED WHEN CHEWED. HE TRIED AND TRIED AND FINALLY FOUND THE RIGHT MIXTURE THAT COULD BE USED TO BLOW HUGE, NONSTICKING BUBBLES. DUBBLE BUBBLE WAS BORN!

PLAY BALL!

Topps created the perfect match between baseball and bubble gum in 1951 when the company introduced gum packaged with baseball cards. The first series featured two individual sets of 52 cards each. The following year there were larger cards that included baseball statistics, team logos, and personal information about and color photos of the players.

Topps holds the record for making the world's largest piece of bubble gum. They took a hunk of Bazooka brand gum equal to l0,000 pieces and presented it to baseball player Willie Mays in 1974. Mays chopped it into smaller chunks and gave it away to children in nearby hospitals.

THE ART OF BLOWING BUBBLES

YES, WE'RE SURE YOU CAN CHEW GUM AND WALK AT THE SAME TIME, BUT CAN YOU BLOW A GOOD BUBBLE?

STEP 1. CHEW A FRESH PIECE OF GUM UNTIL IT'S NICE AND SOFT. ACTUALLY, YOU WANT TO CHEW THE SUGAR OUT OF YOUR GUM. SUGAR GIVES IT FLAVOR, BUT SUGAR DOESN'T STRETCH, AND IT CAN CAUSE A BUBBLE TO COLLAPSE EARLY. MUSH THE GUM AROUND WITH YOUR TONGUE TO MAKE IT PLIABLE. YOUR GOAL IS TO GET A WELL-BLENDED, UN-SUGARY LAYER OF GUM IN THE FRONT OF YOUR MOUTH.

STEP 2. KEEP THE THICKNESS OF YOUR GUM CONSISTENT. REALLY STICK YOUR TONGUE OUT AND GET A BIG BUBBLE POCKET ON TOP. MAKE AS LARGE AN OPENING AS POSSIBLE TO BLOW THROUGH, AND BLOW EVENLY.

FUN FACT: The biggest bubble ever was blown by Susan Montgomery Williams of Fresno, California, on April 19, 1985. It measured 22 inches (56 cm) in diameter, according to the <u>Guinness Book of World Records.</u>

SHHHHH! ON THE CHEWING GUM ASSEMBLY LINE

Gum's the word at the chewing gum factory because each manufacturer has its own secret recipe.

But all gum has five main ingredients: gum base, sugar, corn syrup, softeners, and flavoring.

Gum base is usually a mixture of synthetic (artificially manufactured) and natural materials. Gum base does not dissolve during chewing, and it's what keeps gum springy for hours.

WHY DID THE CHEWING GUM CROSS THE ROAD?

THE CHICKEN HAD STEPPED IN IT!

WHAT DOES A WHALE CHEW?

BLUBBER GUM.

WHAT DO YOU CALL A WILD WEST OUTLAW WHO BURSTS HIS ENEMY'S BUBBLES?

A GUM SLINGER.

STICKY PROBLEMS

WHAT HAPPENS IF YOU SWALLOW GUM?
Nothing — although we don't recommend it! Gum passes harmlessly through your digestive system in one to three days.

HOW DO YOU GET CHEWING GUM OFF THINGS?
Gum has been the curse of parents, teachers, bosses, and cleaning staffs throughout the world who have scraped it off seats, desks, sidewalks, and trees.

If gum sticks to your face, pat it with the rest of the gum to get it off. If gum gets stuck in your hair, rub a little peanut butter or mayonnaise on the area to soften the gum up, and then slide it off. Don't forget to shampoo.

If gum gets stuck to your clothing or furniture, rub an ice cube over the gum. When the gum hardens and starts to crumble, gently scrape it off with a dull knife.

WHY DOES GUM GO HARD AFTER YOU'VE CHEWED IT?
If you've ever felt a disgusting blob of someone else's gum under your desk, you know it's hard as a rock. That's because the softeners that keep gum pliable by helping it hold in moisture are gone. As you chew gum, you also chew the softeners out of it. When you take gum out of your mouth, all the moisture evaporates — and you're left with hard gum sculptures!

RAIN FOREST CHICLEROS

Once upon a time all chewing gum was made from chicle. That's the milky latex of the sapodilla tree, a tropical evergreen native to the rain forests of Central and South America.

The sap was collected by "chicleros," or chicle workers, who climbed up the tall trees and cut zigzags in the trunks with their machetes. The sticky, milky, white sap oozed slowly down the gashes into buckets. Then the chicle was boiled, molded into blocks, and shipped to chewing gum factories. The process of collecting chicle today is very similar to ancient methods and does not harm trees.

Chicle and other latexes are a natural defense mechanism used by trees. The sapodilla produces the gummy sap to protect itself from chewing animals and to repair wounds to its bark.

Today most gum bases are synthetic. By taking the chicle out of our gum, we no longer support a renewable rain forest industry when we chew. Sapodilla sapping, which does not destroy the tree, is a forest-friendly method of production.

FINICKY FACTS ABOUT THE CHEWING-GUM TREE

The sapodilla (*Achras sapota*) tree usually cannot be tapped until it is 70 years old.

The latex of the tree only flows well in the rainy season, from June to February.

The chewing-gum tree will run latex only during the daytime — the drips stop at sunset and begin again at sunrise.

After tapping, the tree has to rest for four to eight years before it can be tapped again.

The sapodilla is one of the tallest trees in the rain forests of Central and South America, attaining a height of more than 100 feet (35 m) and a diameter of up to 4 feet (over 1 m).

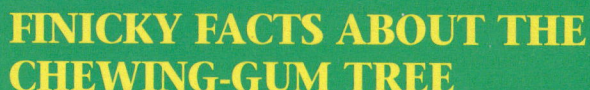

Rainforests are dense, steamy forests that grow in the tropics where it is very hot and rains almost everyday. The trees reach such enormous heights that they actually affect the weather.

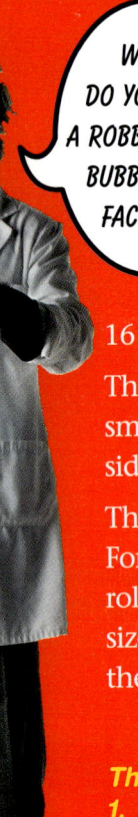

"WHAT DO YOU CALL A ROBBERY AT A BUBBLE GUM FACTORY?"

MEANWHILE, BACK AT THE PLANT...

In a modern-day chewing gum factory, the gum bases, which are synthetic or natural, are melted together in a large kettle and mixed with sugar and corn syrup until a thick syrup is formed.

When the gum is the right consistency, flavoring and colors are added. Usually the mixture is 20 percent gum base, 63 percent sugar, 16 percent corn syrup, and 1 percent flavoring oils.

The blended gum is cooled on belts and kneaded by machines until it has a smooth, even texture. Powdered sugar (or sugar substitute) is sprinkled on both sides to prevent the gum from sticking to the machines.

The gum is formed into the appropriate shapes. For sticks, the gum is passed through a sheet-rolling machine, thinly flattened, and cut to size. Machines wrap the sticks separately and then bundle them into sealed packages.

"A STICKY SITUATION!"

The three largest gum manufacturers are:
1. William Wrigley Jr. Co.
2. Warner-Lambert Co. (American Chicle)
3. Life Savers Co.

NOT-SO-FUN GUM FACTS

● In Singapore, chewing gum is so taboo that the mere possession of it is punishable by a year in jail.

● In the Netherlands, the use of dry-ice jet guns originally designed to clean aircraft parts has been adapted by the government to blast off the millions of gobs of chewing gum that are stuck to the streets. The Dutch people consume about 11 million pounds (5 million kg) of gum annually — about 13 packs per person!

● In the U.S. in the late 1800s, many people "tsk-tsked" the gum chewing habit. If you were caught chewing in school, a teacher might rap your knuckles hard with a ruler. And scientists who looked down on this diversion spread false rumors that chicle was a mixture of horses' hooves and glue.

● If you accidentally swallowed gum, some naysayers said, your intestines would stick together, causing death. This is not true!

Peppermint is the most popular flavor of gum worldwide.

WHAT IS A "GUM GAME"?

A TRICK INTENDED TO CHEAT A VICTIM. THE EXPRESSION COMES FROM THE OBSERVATION THAT OPOSSUMS AND RACCOONS OFTEN HIDE IN A SWEET GUM TREE WHEN HUNTED.

BUBBLE, BUBBLE, TOIL AND TROUBLE: GUM EXPERIMENTS

1. HOW LONG DOES THE FLAVOR REALLY LAST?

What you need: One clock. CHEW ON THIS! gum plus two other standard brands of chewing gum in the same flavor.

What you do: Hide the labels of the three brands of gum. Copy the chart below to record your results. Predict how long you think the flavor will last for each piece of gum. Chew with the same force; chew on both sides of your mouth; keep your mouth closed while chewing.

What happens: The flavor starts to disappear the instant you put a piece of chewing gum into your mouth because saliva washes off the sugary coating. Then, as you chew, saliva dissolves the sweet flavoring. It won't dissolve the gum base, though, and so eventually you're left with a rubbery lump!

MINUTES FLAVOR LASTS

Brand	Prediction	Test 1	Test 2	Test 3	Average

2. IS CHEWING GUM BIODEGRADABLE?

Ione Lavalle conducted a secret experiment when she was 14 years old. She decided to test the destructibility of gum. She blew a bubble and attached it to a low branch of a tree. She checked it out after a day, a week, a month, and a year, and it actually survived three years — even through a brutal and challenging Minnesota winter.

Take a piece of gum and do the same thing: Blow a big bubble and fasten it securely to a tree. Check on it periodically. Is it still there? Has it become smaller? Has it changed texture or form? Did it withstand changes in the weather?

What happens: With time and exposure to the elements, all things on Earth decompose, biodegrade, or somehow change — and that includes chewing gum. But how long does it take?

3. WHO'S THE BEST BUBBLE MAKER?

What you need: Two friends. A pack of chewing gum.

What you do: Put the gum in your mouth, moisten it, and get ready to blow.

Rate your bubbles:

1. Who can blow the cutest bubble?
2. Who can blow the smallest bubble? The biggest?
3. Who can blow the weirdest bubble?
4. Who can make the loudest pop?
5. Who can make the most annoying cracking sound?

TO CHEW OR NOT TO CHEW?

WHAT IS A "GUMMER"?

AN OLD SHEEP THAT HAS LOST ALL ITS TEETH!

WHEN YOU CHEW GUM, CAN YOU REALLY SHOUT..."LOOK, MA, NO CAVITIES"?

Here's what dentists think: When you chew gum you increase the flow of saliva, which is a good thing because it helps neutralize traces of acid that may cause tooth decay. However, the sugar in gum isn't so great because the bacteria in your mouth digest the sugar to make acid, which attacks the enamel of teeth and makes a cavity. Whew!

When you chew sugarless gum it brings more saliva to your mouth without adding any sugar, and so it slows the effects of harmful bacteria. It's actually an acceptable way to fight cavities.

Some dentists think that when you chew sugared gum the saliva that your mouth produces washes the sugar from the gum into your stomach fairly quickly, before the acid can do much damage to your teeth.

You be the judge: just remember that moderation is the key.

DON'T SHARE GUM WITH YOUR DOG... AND OTHER PIECES OF GUM ETIQUETTE

POP! CRACKLE!

RULE NO. 1: DON'T SHARE GUM WITH YOUR FRIENDS, SIBLINGS, OR PETS BECAUSE THERE ARE GERMS LURKING EVERYWHERE.

RULE NO. 2: DON'T TAKE THE GUM FROM YOUR MOUTH AND PUT IT SOMEPLACE ELSE — LIKE UNDER THE TABLE OR IN YOUR SISTER'S HAIR.

RULE NO. 3: DON'T LET OTHER PEOPLE HEAR THE CRACKLE AND POP OF YOUR GUM. CHEW IN SILENCE WITH YOUR MOUTH CLOSED.

Sharing someone's ABC (already–been–chewed) gum is sometimes thought to be a sign of true love, as Tom Sawyer proved when he shared a piece with Becky Thatcher.

RULE NO. 4: MASTER THE ART OF DISPOSING OF GUM. PLEASE DON'T STICK IT ON A DINNER PLATE OR UNDER THE TABLE. REMEMBER THAT IT'S RUDE TO SPIT IT OUT ON THE STREET OR SIDEWALK WHERE AN UNSUSPECTING PERSON COULD STEP ON IT.

RULE NO. 5: SHARE AND SHARE ALIKE: IF YOU HAVE A PACK OF GUM, MAKE SURE THERE'S ENOUGH FOR EVERYONE. AND IF YOU ONLY HAVE ONE STICK, OFFER HALF TO YOUR FRIEND.

HOW TO REPAIR AN AIRPLANE...
AND OTHER USES FOR CHEWING GUM!

UNBELIEVABLE!

1. CRIME STOPPER
Dr. William Alexander, a dentist from Oregon, has used gum to capture criminals. In one murder case, a suspect claimed he was not at the scene of the crime. Chewed gum had been found there by a police officer. The dentist took an impression of the suspect's mouth and compared it with the bite marks on the gum. The bite marks matched the impression exactly. Case closed.

2. PIPE REPAIR
In 1988 a New York preschooler rammed a toy fire engine into a gas pipe and caused a dangerous leak. But his ingenious 12-year-old baby-sitter kept cool and plugged the leak with a wad

of bubble gum.

3. BUG STOPPER Some gardeners who don't like to use chemicals to kill bugs use liquid bubble gum instead. The bugs are attracted to the bubble gum and try to eat it. But when they do their jaws stick shut, making garden plants safe from their bites.

4. AIRPLANE REPAIR Chewing gum was used to patch a hole in the water jacket of the engine of a British Royal Air Force dirigible while it was crossing the Atlantic Ocean to the U.S. in 1911.

COOL DUDE!

Why was the detective so good at blowing bubbles?
He was a gumshoe.

What is a "gumshoe"?
A rubber overshoe. The word became a slang expression for a detective.

Why are detectives called "gumshoes"?

a) They stick to a case until it is solved.

b) When they patrol the streets, they pick up chewing gum on their shoes.

c) The rubber soles of their shoes don't make any noise, so they can tiptoe around to get clues.

[The answer is c.]

29

MAKE YOUR OWN BUBBLE GUM!

The CHEW ON THIS! kit includes:
- pellets of gum base
- pouch of corn syrup
- package of flavored sugar mixture
- plastic tray
- wooden stick for stirring

A safety reminder:
Making chewing gum is an activity for adults and children to do together. Before you start, ask your mom, your dad, or another grown-up to help you. Your grown-up helper can show you the safe way to take things out of the microwave or oven, using oven mitts or pot holders. Always be very careful when you are around a stove or microwave oven. Never handle anything hot with your bare hands.

CAUTION: The gum base and corn syrup mixture will be very hot. Handle with care.

What you do:

1. Pour the sugar mixture onto a kitchen counter or cutting board. Form it into a mound.

2. Spread the gum pellets evenly in the plastic tray.

3. Cut the end of the corn syrup pouch and squeeze the corn syrup evenly over the gum pellets in the tray.

4. **Microwave ovens:** Place the tray in the center of the oven. Microwave uncovered, on HIGH (100%), for 30 seconds. Check the mixture to see if the gum pellets have melted, and flattened. If not, microwave again, 15 seconds at a time, until the mixture is melted. This should not take more than 2 minutes. **Do not leave the microwave unattended while cooking this mixture. Overcooking may cause scorching.**

Conventional ovens: Preheat the oven to 325°F (165°C). Place the tray on a baking pan in the center of the oven. Bake the mixture for 4 minutes. If the gum pellets have not melted, bake for up to 6 additional minutes, checking every 2 minutes until melted. The tray will be very hot.

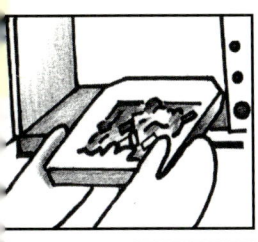
5. Wear oven mitts or use pot holders to remove the tray from the microwave or oven.

6. Use the wooden stick to stir the gum pellets and corn syrup together until they are well mixed. Some corn syrup may be left over.

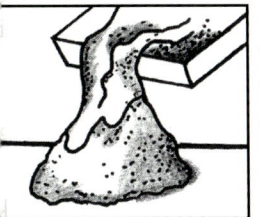
7. Pour the gum mixture into the center of the mound of sugar mixture. Let the gum mixture cool for 1 minute.

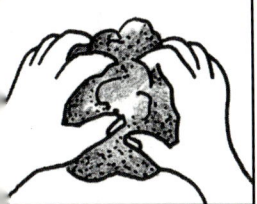
8. Knead the gum and the sugar mixtures together for 3 to 4 minutes, until they are well combined, and the gum is no longer sticky. All the sugar mixture will probably not be used.

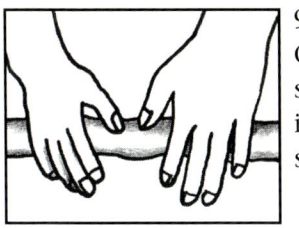
9. Divide the kneaded gum in half. Coat your hands with the left over sugar mixture. Roll the kneaded gum into two long snakes. Let the gum stand for 10 minutes.

10. Use a knife to slice the gum into bite-sized pieces. Use the gum right away, or put it in a self-sealing bag, and store it in a cool place.

MAKE YOUR OWN GUM WRAPPERS!

- Have fun designing wrappers for your chewing gum!
- Think up a clever name!
- Use the patterns provided on the next page or be creative and design your own!

31

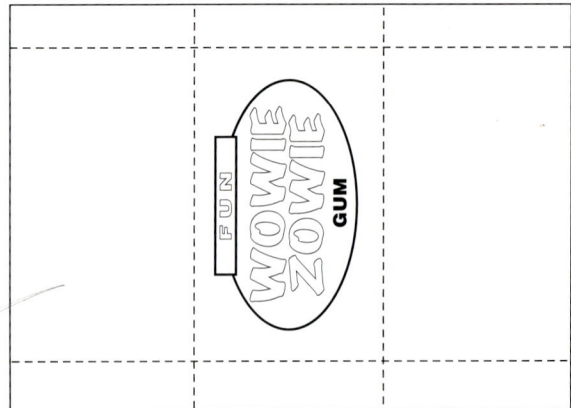

Design #1.
1. Trace or make photocopies of the artwork.
2. Color the artwork with your markers or pencil crayons. Cut out the wrappers.
3. Cut the gum into strips 3" x 3/4" (7.5 cm x 2 cm) and wrap the pieces in tinfoil.
4. Wrap the wrappers around the tinfoil-covered pieces, letting the ends show.

Design #2.
1. Trace or make photocopies of the artwork.
2. Color the artwork with your markers or pencil crayons. Cut out the wrappers.
3. Cut the gum into strips 1 1/2" x 1" (4 cm x 2.5 cm)
4. Wrap the package wrapper around the pieces.